Silky the Fairy enters the Land of Mine-All-Mine from the Faraway Tree looking for adventure. She has visited many Lands in search of fun and excitement. But when she meets Talon the evil Troll she soon finds that her Enchanted World is turned upside down.

To rescue the Talismans that have been lost from the Faraway Tree, Silky will need some help, and fast! Luckily she can rely on her best fairy friends to help her in her task. With the special talents of Melody, Petal, Pinx and Bizzy, Silky must save the Lands of the Enchanted World. But will the fairies succeed or will Talon get his evil way?

EGMONT
We bring stories to life

Silky and the Everlasting Candle
Published in Great Britain 2009
by Egmont UK Limited
239 Kensington High Street, London W8 6SA

Text and illustrations
ENID BLYTON® ENID BLYTON'S ENCHANTED WORLD™
Copyright © 2009 Chorion Rights Limited.
All rights reserved.

Text by Elise Allen
Illustrations by Dynamo

ISBN 978 1 4052 4674 3

1 3 5 7 9 10 8 6 4 2

A CIP catalogue record for this title is available from the British Library

Printed and bound in Great Britain by the CPI Group

Enid Blyton's ENCHANTED WORLD

Silky and the Everlasting Candle

By Elise Allen

EGMONT

Meet the Faraway Fairies

Favourite Colour – Yellow. It's a beautiful colour that reminds me of sunshine and happiness.

Talent – Light. I can release rays of energy to light up a room or, if I really try hard, I can use it to break out of tight situations. The only problem is that when I lose my temper I can have a 'flash attack' which is really embarrassing because my friends find it funny.

Favourite Activity – Exploring. I love an adventure, even when it gets me into trouble. I never get tired of visiting new places and meeting new people.

Favourite Colour – Blue. The colour of the sea and the sky. I love every shade from aquamarine to midnight blue.

Talent – As well as being a musician I can also transform into other objects. I like to do it for fun, but it also comes in useful if there's a spot of bother.

Favourite Activity – Singing and dancing. I can do it all day and never get tired.

Favourite Colour – Green. It's the colour of life. All my best plant friends are one shade of green or another.

Talent – I can speak to the animals and plants of the Enchanted World . . . not to mention the ones in the Faraway Tree.

Favourite Activity – I love to sit peacefully and listen to the constant chatter of all creatures, both big and small.

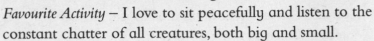

Favourite Colour – Pink. What other colour would it be? Pink is simply the best colour there is.

Talent – Apart from being a supreme fashion designer, I can also become invisible. It helps me to escape from my screaming fashion fans!

Favourite Activity – Designing. Give me some fabrics and I'll make you something fabulous. Remember – If it's not by Pinx . . . your makeover stinks!

Favourite Colour – Orange. It's the most fun colour of all. It's just bursting with life!

Talent – Being a magician of course. Although I have been known to make the odd Basic Bizzy Blunder with my spells.

Favourite Activity – Baking Brilliant Blueberry Buns and Marvellous Magical Muffins. There is always time to bake a tasty cake to show your friends that you care.

www.blyton.com/enchantedworld

Contents

Introduction

*T*ucked away among the thickets, groves and
forests of our Earth is a special wood. An
Enchanted Wood, where the trees grow taller, the
branches grow stronger and the leaves grow denser
than anywhere else. Search hard enough within this
Enchanted Wood, and you'll find one tree that
towers above all the others. This is the Faraway Tree,
and it is very special. It is home to magical creatures
like elves and fairies, even a dragon. But the most
magical thing about this very magical Tree? It is the
sole doorway to the Lands of the Enchanted World.

Most of the time, the Lands of the Enchanted
World simply float along, unattached to anything.
But at one time or another, they each come to rest at

the top of the Faraway Tree. And if you're lucky enough to be in the Tree at the time, you can climb to its very top, scramble up the long Ladder extending from its tallest branch, push through the clouds and step into that Land.

Of course, there's no telling when a Land will come to the Faraway Tree, or how long it will remain. A Land might stay for months, or be gone within the hour. And if you haven't made it back down the Ladder and into the Faraway Tree before the Land floats away, you could be stuck for a very long time. This is scary even in the most wonderful of Lands, like the Land of Perfect Birthday Parties. But if you get caught in a place like the Land of Ravenous Toothy Beasts, the situation is absolutely terrifying. Yet even though exploring the Lands has its perils, it's also exhilarating, which is why creatures from all over the Enchanted World (and the occasional visiting human) come to live in the Faraway Tree so they can travel from Land to Land.

Of course, not everyone explores the Lands for

pleasure alone. In fact, five fairies have been asked do so for the ultimate cause: to save the life of the Faraway Tree and make sure the doorway to the Enchanted World remains open. These are their stories . . .

Chapter One
Zuni's Surprise

'Hah!' Zuni cried triumphantly. 'I beat you again!'

The handsome, silver-haired sylvite boy was breathing heavily as he spoke but couldn't keep the grin off his face.

'Best of seven?' asked Silky the Fairy, also gasping for air.

The two best friends had been racing across the breadth of the Faraway Tree all afternoon and were now beginning to get tired.

'What are you, a glutton for punishment?' Zuni laughed. 'I've already beaten you three times today!'

'And I beat you twice,' Silky countered. 'I'd say we're pretty evenly matched. We need four out of seven to know for sure.'

'OK then,' Zuni grinned, and he and Silky took their starting positions, both holding on to the far end of the furthest branch. 'On your marks . . . get set . . . GO!'

The two soared off across the sky . . . well, at least Silky did, since she was the one with wings. Yet Zuni's lack of wings only put him at the slightest disadvantage. He was an astounding athlete and swung easily from branch to branch, turning double and triple somersaults as he weaved through the Tree. The two raced neck and neck across the vast canopy of leaves and branches: Silky ducking and zigzagging to avoid the obstacles; Zuni swinging, jumping and climbing, using it all to his advantage.

They both grinned happily as they raced, loving the feeling of the wind rushing into their faces and the thrill of pushing each other to their limit. Perfectly matched, it was

impossible to split the pair – until the very last second when Silky used her last scrap of energy to pull ahead by a whisker.

'YES!' she cried. 'I beat you! That's three each – one more decides it all!'

'You're crazy!' Zuni panted. 'We've been up here all day. I have to get back and feed Misty.'

'What's the matter, Zuni?' Silky taunted him. 'Are you afraid you'll lose again?'

'No,' Zuni assured her. 'I'm just exhausted . . . aren't you?'

Silky *was* absolutely exhausted, but she couldn't admit that to Zuni. She was up here on a mission to distract Zuni for as long as possible so that Petal, Melody, Pinx, Bizzy and Misty the Unicorn could decorate the treehouse and prepare it for Zuni's surprise birthday party. Then Silky was supposed to bring Zuni to the treehouse, where the celebration would begin. It was possible the other fairies were ready, but just in case they weren't . . .

'I know what it is,' Silky said playfully. 'You just get tired faster because you don't have wings.'

Silky meant it as a joke, a tease to get Zuni to race again. She certainly didn't mean to upset him. All sylvites were athletic, but none had ever possessed the skill of Zuni, who could leap, run, dive and climb better than anyone Silky had ever seen, even in the Land of Olympians. Although he had no wings, Silky knew that Zuni was on more than an equal footing with her. He had already beaten her across the canopy three times.

But Zuni didn't take Silky's comment as a joke at all. A shadow fell over his face, and he turned his dark blue eyes away from her.

'I can't believe you'd say that,' Zuni muttered softly.

'What?' Silky asked, stunned that her

comment had hurt him. Couldn't he tell she was joking? 'Zuni, I was just –'

'You know that's the reason Witch Whisper won't let me go on the Talisman missions,' Zuni snapped, cutting her off. 'I don't have wings, so she thinks I'll slow you down.'

'But Zuni, she's just being careful,' Silky replied. 'It's not because you couldn't –'

'She's not being that careful,' Zuni said bitterly. 'She's not worried about five fairies stumbling through the Enchanted World. Just me – the one who can't fly.'

Now it was Silky's turn to be affronted. '"Stumbling around the Enchanted World!" Since I've been here, I have travelled to every Land that's come to the top of the Tree, and never once have I "stumbled" anywhere. Just because I'm not a boy doesn't mean that I can't do some good in the Enchanted World. You should know that better than anyone!'

'Forget it,' Zuni said, cutting her off. 'I'll see

*** 9 ***

you later.' And he darted off, expertly tumbling his way back down the Tree.

'Zuni, I'm talking to you!' Silky objected, and flew down after him. But this time Zuni used all his acrobatic skill to quickly spin and soar through the branches of the Tree until he was out of sight.

Silky screamed in frustration, releasing a burst of light that flew back up into the Tree's branches and hit the home of Dame Washalot, who gave a startled squeal and tipped out her bucket of dirty washing water . . . all over Silky!

Soaked and cold, Silky suddenly realised what a mess she had made of things. It was Zuni's birthday. She was supposed to be preparing him for a fabulous surprise, and instead she had hurt his feelings, then lost her temper. And what could she do now? Zuni could be anywhere in the Faraway Tree, and Silky knew him well enough to be sure that if he didn't want to be found, she'd never spot him. Abashed, she flew back to the treehouse to tell the other fairies what had happened.

'SURPRISE!' cried Petal, Melody, Pinx and Bizzy when Silky opened the treehouse door.

The main room of the treehouse had been decorated beautifully in layers of multicoloured fabric and flowers in Zuni's honour. As Melody led the fairies in a spirited version of *Happy Birthday To You*, Misty the Unicorn danced through the air with a giant birthday cake balanced on her back. The top tier was made of confetti cake and, as the song ended, it exploded, raining a blizzard of pastel-coloured confetti everywhere.

'What happened to you?' Pinx asked, suddenly realising that Silky was dripping dirty water all over the floor and did not have Zuni with her.

'I messed up,' Silky admitted, closing the door. But before she could say anything more, there was a knock at the door. Silky smiled

hopefully. 'Maybe that's Zuni!' she said.

'Ooh! Places, everyone!' Melody whispered.

With a flourish of her wand, Bizzy returned the confetti to the top layer of the cake, which magically reconstructed itself. Quickly, Misty and the fairies soared into the corners of the room. When they were all set, Silky cried, 'Come in!'

The door opened.

The fairies immediately burst into song, Misty did her dance, and the cake exploded once again, raining confetti everywhere . . . confetti that landed on a rather confused Cluecatcher and Witch Whisper.

When the fairies realised who had actually entered, they gasped. The look on Cluecatcher's and Witch Whisper's face told the fairies that there could only be one reason for their visit.

'There's a new Land at the top of the Tree,' Petal said. Cluecatcher nodded in confirmation and the fairies gathered around him.

'The Land of Birthdays,' Cluecatcher said solemnly. 'Where every day is a birthday celebration.'

'The Land of Birthdays,' Melody echoed in delight. 'That sounds like the most wonderful Land ever!'

'Yes . . . but that's what we said about Sleepover Land too,' Bizzy said, and Melody went quiet, remembering how strange their last adventure had actually been.

'The Talisman for the Land of Birthdays is the Everlasting Candle,' Witch Whisper told the fairies. 'A birthday candle that never melts, no matter how long it stays lit, and can neither be snuffed nor blown out.'

'Never be blown out? How frustrating – your wish would never come true!' Pinx turned to the other fairies. 'Promise you'll never put that candle on my birthday cake.'

'I don't think that will be a problem, Pinx,' Silky laughed. 'It's nowhere near your birthday.'

'Or any of your birthdays,' Witch Whisper added. 'Which could be a problem. You can't enter the Land of Birthdays unless you are accompanied by someone celebrating a birthday.'

'Then how can we possibly get up there to find the Talisman?' Petal asked.

Suddenly, the door burst open and Zuni walked into the treehouse. Eleven pairs of eyes (including Cluecatcher's four pairs) locked on Zuni immediately, but the sylvite didn't seem to notice them. He walked straight to Silky and stood in front of her. A lock of silver hair fell over his face, and he pushed it aside so that he could meet his friend's eyes.

'I'm sorry, Silky,' he said. 'I acted horribly before, and I didn't mean any of it. You've never stumbled through anything. None of you have –'

But he stopped mid-sentence, noticing the other four fairies, Witch Whisper, Cluecatcher and Misty for the first time – along with the half-exploded cake and the confetti that still decorated every surface. He also couldn't help but notice everyone's expectant grins.

'What's going on?' Zuni asked.

Silky's smile spread even wider as she took her friend's hand.

'Zuni. I believe we're about to give you the best birthday present you have ever had.'

Chapter Two
The New Talisman Team

Zuni's mouth curled into an amused smirk as he pulled one of the many pieces of confetti from Silky's blonde hair. 'Will I need an umbrella?' he asked warily.

'Not in the Land of Birthdays,' Witch Whisper observed. 'The weather is always beautiful there. Nothing ever goes amiss. It hasn't rained in its entire history.'

'What?' Zuni asked, and turned to Witch Whisper, confused.

Silky squeezed his hand to get his attention back. She looked him in the eye and leaned in close, barely able to contain her excitement. 'Zuni,' she began, 'how would you like to come with us on our next Talisman mission?'

Zuni's eyebrows scrunched together

questioningly as he looked from Silky to Witch Whisper and Cluecatcher, and then to the other fairies. The slightest hint of a blush rose in his cheeks, and he lowered his silver lashes. 'You don't have to do this,' he muttered softly to Silky. 'I mean, I know what I said before, but –'

'Silky is not taking pity on you, Zuni,' Witch Whisper assured him. 'She needs you. The fairies can't get into the Land of Birthdays without someone who is celebrating a birthday.'

'Really?' Zuni asked. His entire face brightened with the possibility, but a second later he frowned. He jutted out his chin and fixed Witch Whisper with a challenging gaze. 'But I thought you said I couldn't go on missions because I'd slow the others down. You know . . . since I don't have wings.'

Witch Whisper held back a smile. 'You *could* slow them down,' she admitted. 'But without you there *is* no mission. I would say that makes you fairly indispensible, wouldn't you?'

'YES!' Bizzy cried, unable to contain her excitement a moment longer. 'You're the Crux of our Candle Crusade!'

'What?' Zuni laughed as Bizzy and the other fairies swarmed around him, all eager to share their enthusiasm.

'*Please* come with us, Zuni,' Melody said. 'It will make the mission so special.'

'And, Zuni, the creatures in these Lands . . . you won't believe it,' Petal gushed. 'I can't wait to meet them with you.'

'Come on, it's not like I've never been to other Lands,' Zuni gently reminded her. But he was smiling as he said it because he knew exactly what Petal meant.

The two of them had been very close since she had first arrived in the Faraway Tree and used her powers to translate Misty the Unicorn's neighs, whinnies and snorts for Zuni.

Zuni and Misty had been inseparable ever since the sylvite had rescued the orphaned foal from the Land of Mythical Beasts. He had always felt like he understood Misty's every thought, but it was incredible for him to hear what she was *actually* saying, and it had made him and Petal firm friends immediately.

Since then, the three had spent countless hours together, with Petal translating not only for Misty, but for all the creatures in the area. Experiencing a new Land with Petal would be unlike anything Zuni had ever known, and he was just as thrilled by the idea as she was.

'Well, there's one creature you'll meet that you've *never* seen,' Pinx said, wrinkling her nose at the thought. 'Talon.'

Bizzy giggled. 'Unless he's still getting a Magnificently Monstrous Makeover from the sleepees.'

The fairies laughed, remembering the last time they saw the awful Troll: swallowed up to his neck by Sleepover Land while groups of young girls plaited his hair and painted his face with shimmery make-up.

Silky caught Witch Whisper's eye, and the witch's raised brow told Silky exactly what she was thinking.

'He always gets away though,' Silky sighed. 'Remember the Land of Giants? He escaped *and* he got his crystal back from wherever he hid it.'

'But even if he did escape the sleepees,' Petal mused, 'he can't get into the Land of Birthdays, right? Not unless it's *his* birthday.'

Pinx snorted. 'A Talon the Troll birthday party. Can you *imagine*? The colour scheme alone would be disgusting: all toad-green and rotten-wart black. And think of the party games –'

'It's *not* Talon's birthday,' Witch Whisper cut her off sharply. Her tone was unusually stern, and Silky had the feeling there was a story behind it, but she didn't get the chance to ask before Bizzy leaped in.

'You mean it's a Totally Talon-less Talisman Task?' she squealed.

'In the Land of Birthdays!' Melody crowed.

'And with Zuni!' Petal added.

'It's official,' Pinx declared. 'This is going to be the most incredible mission ever.'

Silky agreed. She took both of Zuni's hands and looked him in the eye again, her whole being bubbling over with excitement. 'Please, Zuni,' she implored. 'Please say you'll come with us.'

Zuni looked at the five fairies, all genuinely ecstatic about the idea of him joining them. Zuni couldn't even *try* to play it cool. This was the chance he had been waiting for, ever since the missions had begun, and he felt his mouth spread into an overjoyed grin that mirrored the fairies' own. 'You know,' he smiled at Silky, 'we never did our best of seven tiebreaker.'

Silky's eyes lit up as she returned his smile. 'Race you to the Ladder?'

In the blink of an eye, both Silky and Zuni were gone, zipping out of the treehouse and flying and leaping until they reached the very top of the Faraway Tree. Breathlessly, the two friends lunged for the bottom rung. By a hair, Silky's hand smacked against it first.

'I won!' Silky shouted, then flew back from the Ladder a little, presenting it to Zuni with a sweep of her arms. 'After you,' she grinned.

Zuni reached out to start climbing the Ladder when . . .

'STOP! Wait for us!' Pinx gasped.

Zuni and Silky looked down to see Pinx, Bizzy, Petal and Melody approaching, all with matching flushed faces and panting for breath.

'Sorry,' winced Zuni. 'I guess we got a little carried away.'

'Not at all!' cried Bizzy. 'It's your first mission! We just don't want to miss a single second!'

A moment later, all the fairies had caught up, and the whole group stood together at the bottom of the Ladder.

'Go ahead, Zuni,' Petal encouraged. 'Lead the way.'

Zuni smiled at his friends who were all grinning back at him in eager anticipation. 'Here goes nothing,' he shrugged, and he climbed on to the lowest rung of the Ladder. A bolt of energy thrilled through him, and he raced upwards, faster and faster, the fairies flying right behind him . . . until he suddenly stopped short, stunned by the most disgusting odour he had ever smelled.

'Whoa!' he shouted, nearly falling off the Ladder in disgust. 'Is it always like this?'

'If it were, do you think we'd still go on these missions? Urgh!' Pinx lifted the neck of her T-shirt over her nose so she wouldn't have to inhale the hideous stench that whooshed down the Ladder, bathing the group in the sickening aroma of rotting fish, overcooked broccoli and mouldy feet.

Then suddenly it was gone, and Zuni and the fairies could breathe again.

'Nasty,' Zuni winced. 'I've never smelled anything like that.'

'We have,' Silky realised, her eyes widening. 'We smell it every time we get too close to Talon.'

Everyone was silent for a moment. Could Talon really be nearby?

Then Pinx laughed. 'We're being ridiculous!

Has Talon *ever* appeared without screaming, stamping and destroying everything in his path? If he were around, we wouldn't just smell him – we'd see and hear him as well!

The fairies had to admit that was true. Subtlety had never been Talon's strong point. His personality demanded that he make a grand entrance wherever he went. It was silly to think that he would ever sneak by the fairies unnoticed. The smell was certainly as horrible as Talon, but that didn't mean it was him. It could have been from anything, really. Surely it was nothing to worry about.

'So, if that's all settled,' Zuni began, his eyes dancing with excitement, 'I say we get ourselves to the Land of Birthdays and start our mission. Everyone with me?' Zuni's grin was as contagious as his enthusiasm, and the fairies eagerly zipped up to the top of the Ladder with him, keen to begin their newest adventure.

Chapter Three

The Perfect Birthday Party

Pitch black.

Most of the time when the fairies reached the top of the Ladder, they simply pushed through a thick layer of clouds and they were at their destination. Not this time. This time they were in deep, inky blackness, and when Zuni tried to push through it . . .

'Ow!' he winced, rubbing his head. 'Since when does the Ladder have a ceiling?'

WHOOSH! A loud, metallic scrape resounded beneath them, and Pinx had to leap away as a sheet of metal slid below them. 'And a floor,' she added.

'I don't like this, Silky . . .' Melody worried.

Silky didn't like it either, but she did what she could to make things a little better. Using her power of illumination, she brought a soft glow to the area. Now Zuni and the fairies could see they had ascended not into a new Land, but into a large metallic tube.

'Where are we?' Petal asked, reaching out to feel the cold, unyielding walls.

As if in answer, a robotic voice said, 'Six visitors.' With a motorised whirr, six pairs of tweezers unfolded from the wall and whipped towards the group, too quickly for them to even react.

'OW!' all six of them cried as the tweezers yanked an individual hair off each of their heads then zipped back into the walls. The room glowed with washes of blue and red lights as the robotic voice said, 'Analysing . . . analysing . . .'

Suddenly, the flashing lights stopped and the robotic voice became human and happy as it lilted, 'Analysis complete: it's Zuni the Sylvite's birthday, and his party profile is

Animals, Action and Adventure!'

Immediately, the metallic cylinder burst open, spilling Zuni and the fairies on to the ground at the feet of two figures. The first was a girl, just a little taller than Zuni himself, but next to her stood a creature unlike anything the group had seen before. He was bright blue, and his whole body was a perfectly round ball, out of which grew two giant feet. The only things on his face were two large eyes and a huge, winning smile. He had no other features: no ears; no arms; no nose; no hair.

'Happy Birthday, Zuni!' cried the girl, extending a hand to help him up. 'I'm Caysee, this is Plook, and we're your official Birthday Planners!'

At the sound of his name, the blue ball transformed his entire body into a trumpet, and sounded a fanfare to welcome the group. This was apparently Plook's talent: like a ball of clay, he could quickly mould his body into anything. Yet, unlike Melody when she transformed, Plook always looked somewhat like himself. No matter what his shape, he was always bright blue, and his eyes and mouth were always visible.

As for Caysee, she also had a special ability: her skin changed colour with her emotions, always reflecting her mood. At the moment she was pink with happiness as she raised her arms in the air and shouted, 'Welcome to the Land of Birthdays!'

'Um . . . thanks,' Zuni said, still getting used to this new Land.

'It's like a giant cake!' Melody giggled delightedly. And she was right.

The entire Land of Birthdays resembled a massive, multi-tiered birthday cake, and every level was filled with celebration. Happy commotion was everywhere. Zuni and the fairies saw colourfully uniformed marching bands, troupes of unicycling, cartwheeling and juggling clowns, thousands of bobbing balloons, and magicians pulling endless streams of bright silk scarves from their pockets.

Then there was the food! Cart after cart of the yummiest delights the fairies and Zuni had ever seen: colour-striped candyfloss, caramel-and-chocolate dipped apples and swirling lollipops larger than a sylvite's face.

Zuni and the fairies couldn't even begin to take in all the dizzying joys of the Land of Birthdays before a series of chimes rang out. Caysee gasped, her skin changing to a sparkly blue. 'Oh, goody!' she squealed. 'Top of the Hour Birthday Shower!'

Caysee pointed up to the top layer of the cake-like Land, where something spectacular was clearly about to happen. Everyone on the terraces stopped what they were doing to look.

Zuni and the fairies followed their gaze. As

every musician in the Land played *Happy Birthday To You*, a giant tiered carousel rose from inside the layer and burst out of its top. The carousel held countless figurines: elves, fairies, pixies, ogres, sylvites . . . beautifully lifelike models of nearly every creature in the Enchanted World, all dressed in stunningly vibrant colours.

Zuni and the fairies watched as the figurines sang and danced along with the music, each tier of the carousel spinning in opposite directions. Then, when the song reached its final crescendo, a mountain of confetti exploded into the air, slowly raining

down on everyone in the Land like a light spring shower.

'Wow!' Pinx gaped. 'That is *so* much cooler than what we tried to do in the treehouse.'

'Yes, it's very impressive,' Zuni said in a dismissive tone that took Silky by surprise. Then he turned to Caysee. 'Here's the thing, though: we're on a very important mission –'

A sparkly purple computer strapped to Caysee's wrist suddenly beeped, interupting Zuni. She looked at it and gasped. 'Oh, no! We're running late! Come on!'

'Actually, I'd rather just talk,' Zuni said, but Caysee had already zipped ahead, walking so fast that the fairies had to fly to keep up. Zuni quickly jogged back to her side.

'You aren't listening,' he told Caysee. 'We're here for a reason: to save the Enchanted World. And we demand you tell us everything you know about the Everlasting Candle.'

'*Zuni!*' hissed Silky under her breath. He

was being so rude!

Caysee and Plook didn't seem bothered, nor did they even break stride. Plook answered Zuni's question by changing into the shape of a grinning candle, as Caysee chirped happily, 'You know about the Everlasting Candle too? It wasn't that long ago when it was first found: a candle that never goes out. You'll see it at the daily Sunset Ceremony!'

'What's the Sunset Ceremony?' asked Bizzy, pausing to grab a sample of marshmallow fudge from a nearby food cart.

'During the day, the whole Land is split into individual birthday parties, customised for everyone celebrating their special day,' Caysee answered. 'But, at sunset we all gather on the top tier of the Land for a huge party and the Birthday Friends share a giant cake covered in enough candles for their combined years. Then everyone sings *Happy Birthday To*

You, the Birthday Friends blow out their candles and we have cake and ice cream and play until we fall asleep and start all over again in the morning! The Everlasting Candle is just perfect for our Sunset Ceremony cake. Every night before we sing it's placed right on top.'

'That's really lovely,' Zuni said curtly. 'But I'm afraid you'll have to give the Candle to us.'

Silky shot him a glare – what was *wrong* with him? 'What Zuni *means* to say . . .' Silky began.

But Caysee didn't seem insulted by Zuni at all. In fact, she was giggling. 'Give it to you? But that's so silly! The Everlasting Candle is controlled by The Works. I couldn't give it to you even if I wanted to!'

'The Works?' Petal echoed curiously.

But they had reached their destination, and Caysee grinned as she opened the gate in a large fence.

'Welcome to your party, Zuni!' she declared. 'Custom-made for someone who loves Animals, Action and Adventure!'

Plook formed himself into an arrow pointing inside, and even Zuni could see there would be no more discussion until they entered. They did, and – for a moment – every thought of the Everlasting Candle and their mission was swept from their minds.

Caysee had said the party was perfectly tailored for Zuni, and she was absolutely right. There was a go-kart track, a climbing wall, a bungee-jump, a huge trampoline, stallion ride – even crocodile wrestling! The crocodile in question was, of course, quite friendly but eager to give its opponents a fun match. And it already had opponents: the party was in full swing, filled with Land of Birthday residents of all species, eager to celebrate with Zuni and make his day as memorable as possible.

'Wow . . .' Zuni's mouth hung open. 'This is . . . This is . . .'

'You like it?' bubbled Caysee, turning a happy bright orange at Zuni's obvious delight.

'I don't know what to do first,' Zuni laughed. 'It's all so cool!'

Suddenly, Petal burst out laughing. 'OK, OK, I'll tell him!' she cried, then turned to Zuni, grinning. 'Calvin says he *really* wants to wrestle you.'

'Calvin?' Zuni asked, frowning.

'The crocodile,' Petal explained.

Zuni's eyes gleamed. 'Let's go!'

Immediately, he and Petal raced over to Calvin while several party guests made sure Zuni's other friends had a great time as well: Silky was ushered to the climbing wall, Pinx was pulled into a go-kart, Melody on to the trampoline, and Bizzy was led to the bungee jump. As they took off in separate directions,

Plook changed into a megaphone and Caysee used him to shout, 'Have a great time! Just remember the one rule of the Land of Birthdays: you have to stay with your Birthday Group at all times, OK?'

'OK!' shouted Zuni and the fairies, though they were already breathless from their new adventures. Silky stretched, hoisting herself higher and higher on the wall, Pinx screamed as her go-kart whizzed round the track at high speed, Melody danced pirouettes high in the air at the top of each trampoline bounce, Bizzy whooped with terrified delight as she fell from the bungee platform – it was so hard not to use her wings! As for Zuni and Petal, they laughed with Calvin the Crocodile's playful teasing as he and Zuni remained locked in their wrestle.

The friends could have played all day, but Zuni was determined to make his first mission

a smashing success, and he had an idea. Zuni
had already pinned Calvin for the third time,
and the two wrestlers were taking a break
when Zuni asked Petal to translate a question:
Caysee had said the Everlasting Candle was
controlled by 'The Works' – what did that
mean?

'Calvin says it's the machinery that
controls everything in the Land of Birthdays,'
Petal translated.

'But where is it?' Zuni asked the crocodile.

'How would I get there?'

Calvin pointed a scaly arm to a vent just above the top of the climbing wall. He growled low in his throat, and Petal translated: 'Vents like that one lead to The Works, but they're only there in case of extreme emergency. No one actually goes in there. They say that when living creatures do enter The Works, they never come out.'

'Thanks, Calvin,' Zuni said, then immediately raced off for the climbing wall.

'Zuni, wait!' cried Petal. 'What are you going to do?'

'Relax,' said Zuni, grinning. 'I'm just going to talk to Silky. Then we can make a plan.'

Petal narrowed her eyes a moment, then shrugged. Whatever ideas Zuni might have, she knew Silky would never let him do anything rash.

Zuni knew it too, which is why he tried to zip up the climbing wall so quickly that Silky wouldn't notice him. He already had one hand on the vent above the wall and was about to pull it outwards when Silky's hand landed on his own, holding it down.

'What are you doing?' Silky asked.

Zuni rolled his eyes. He'd hoped to do this on his own. In a quick whisper he said, 'The Everlasting Candle is in The Works and I'm going in to get it.'

'Alone?' Silky whisper-hissed back. 'Zuni, that's *crazy*! You heard Caysee – the rule here is we all have to stay together. And it's dangerous! If we go in, we go in as a group, and we go in with a plan.'

'What if there's no time for that?' Zuni asked. 'While we're planning, the Land of Birthdays could move away from the Tree. You really want that to happen?'

'Of *course* not,' Silky retorted. 'But we'll lose even more time if we have to rescue you from some crazy mess!'

'That's assuming I'll *need* to be rescued,'
Zuni said, an impish smile lighting his face,
'which I won't.'

'Still, Zuni . . .'

'I'll be back,' Zuni promised, 'and I'll have
the Everlasting Candle.'

'No!' Silky protested, but it was no use.
Despite her hand on his, Zuni pulled on the
vent, yanked it open and slipped inside.

WHOOP! WHOOP! WHOOP!

A blaring alarm filled the Land and
everyone looked up at Silky.

'Stop right there!' cried Caysee.

Without a moment to even think, Silky did
the only thing she could; she leaped in after
Zuni, following him into The Works.

Chapter Four
Split Apart

WHOOP! WHOOP! WHOOP!
The alarm continued to throb as Caysee shouted up at Silky, 'STOP!'

As if to echo her order, Plook transformed himself into a big blue exclamation mark.

But Silky was already gone.

'That's it,' Caysee grumbled, her skin now boiling red with frustration as she pounded at the buttons on her purple wrist-computer.

'Whoa, whoa, whoa!' Pinx spluttered, flying quickly to Caysee's side. 'What are you doing with that thing?'

'I'm blowing you out!' Caysee cried. 'You broke the only rule in the Land of Birthdays: The Birthday Group must stay together!'

'Blowing us out?' Pinx asked. 'What does

that mean?'

'It means you'll be sent away from the Land of Birthdays. You're going back home. And you'll be banned from this Land for life.'

'But you can't do that!' Bizzy cried, as she, Melody and Petal joined Pinx by Caysee's side. 'We need to be here to find the Talisman!'

'Please,' Petal urged gently, 'just give us a chance to explain.' She nodded ever so slightly to Melody, who understood immediately, and began to softly hum a beautiful lullaby. Like everyone who heard Melody's beautiful voice, Caysee couldn't help but be enchanted, and the fairies noticed her skin fading from an angry crimson to a peaceful lavender hue.

Even Plook was affected; he morphed into the shape of a fluffy blue cloud and rocked in time to Melody's soothing tune.

Caysee took a deep breath, lowered her wrist and looked at Petal. 'I'm listening,' she said.

'Thank you,' Petal replied and, as Melody continued humming, Petal explained all she could about the fairies' mission, the Talismans and Talon.

'So, you see,' Petal concluded, 'if you blow us out of the Land, we can never find the Talisman.'

Caysee took a moment to think about

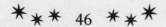

everything Petal had said. 'I understand,' she finally admitted, 'but it's my job to make sure Birthday Groups stay together. Your friends went into The Works and left you. If I don't blow you out, I could get into big trouble.'

'With whom?' Petal asked. 'Who rules the Land of Birthdays? Maybe we could talk to them, and —'

Caysee shook her head. 'The Land is run by The Works.'

'But The Works is a machine,' Petal said. 'Someone has to tell it what to do.'

'Yes,' Caysee admitted, 'but that happened a long time ago. Now The Works handles everything on its own. We Birthday Planners are connected to it through our wrist-pods,' she held out her wrist, showing the purple computer there. 'They tell us what to do: like who's actually having a birthday and can enter the Land, what their birthday profile is, the best party games . . . It even does things on its own, like finding the Everlasting Candle and making it part of the Sunset Ceremony. It runs the whole Land perfectly – as long as we follow all the rules.'

'So what if you break the rules a little?' Pinx challenged her, 'What are you afraid will happen?'

'I don't know,' Caysee fretted, her skin turning yellow. 'No one's ever broken the rules before. We don't do it – we just don't!'

She was clearly getting worked up, and Melody hummed a little louder until Caysee took a deep breath and started to relax again. Still, there was only so much the fairy could do. With Caysee so worried about breaking the rules, there was no real way to keep her from blowing them out of the Land.

'Ooh!' Bizzy piped up. 'Quick Quandary Queller!'

'What?' asked Caysee. She and the rest of the fairies looked at Bizzy, confused.

'It means I have an idea – a solution!'
Bizzy exclaimed. 'What if we went into The
Works too? Once we find our friends, we
won't be breaking the rules, right?'

'No . . .' Caysee admitted, 'you wouldn't . . .
but it's not safe in there.'

'How do you know?' Pinx asked. 'Have
you ever been?'

Caysee paled at the thought. 'No! But
everyone knows it's true. They say living
creatures can't survive inside.'

Pinx shrugged. 'We're willing to take the
risk.'

The fairies could see Caysee was wavering,
but she was worried. Her skin had turned pea
green.

'Please,' Petal urged. 'Think of everything
that's at stake.'

The four fairies looked at Caysee
imploringly, Melody still humming her most
soothing tunes to try and ease her mind.

Finally Caysee nodded.

'OK,' she said, taking a deep breath. 'Since you're trying to find your friends, I won't really be breaking the rules, so I think it'll be all right. But you *must* be together in time for the Sunset Ceremony. If you're not all there at the top of the Land by dusk, there's nothing I can do.' She held out her wrist-computer and said, 'The Works has all your information; it will blow you out itself.'

'We understand,' said Petal. 'Thank you.' Then she turned to her friends. 'That gives us just a few hours.'

'If you can survive that long,' Caysee murmured worriedly, and the fairies realised that the deeper green tinge that had settled into her skin came from fear for their lives.

'We'll be OK,' Melody assured her. 'I promise we'll see you at dusk.'

Caysee didn't seem convinced, but she smiled. Plook couldn't hide his emotions as

well, and he burst into tears, moulding two giant arms from his body to wrap the surprised fairies in a giant hug. When he released them, the group soared up to the vent above the climbing wall.

'Do you really think it's as dangerous inside as they say?' Bizzy asked as Petal pulled open the vent cover.

'I guess we'll find out,' Pinx said as, one by one, they slipped down into The Works.

Chapter Five
Inside The Works

'Zuni, wait!' Silky cried, working to keep the sylvite's shock of silver hair in sight as she flew.

'What's the matter, can't keep up?' Zuni taunted, which only made Silky roll her eyes.

'Hardly,' she muttered, and sped up as she weaved through The Works, the underbelly of the Land of Birthdays. Down here was nothing but the giant machinery that ran the Land: huge mechanisms with moving parts the size of skyscrapers that sliced, pounded and whirred at dizzying speeds.

Petal would hate this place, Silky thought as she dodged the plunging needle of what looked like an enormous sewing machine. *There doesn't seem to be a single living thing down here.* Though the dim lighting allowed her to view everything, there was nothing above, below, or anywhere around her but a vast universe of lifeless, soulless machines pounding repeatedly. *No wonder the residents of the Land of Birthdays fear this place.*

Silky zipped from side to side to avoid a hot iron that slammed down to press several clown costumes. These machines were unforgiving. Make one misjudgement down here and it would surely be your last.

Zuni, however, didn't seem in the least bit intimidated by all the machines, and happily leaped, jumped and swung from one to another as if they were as harmless and familiar as branches in the Faraway Tree. With a final burst of energy, Silky caught up with him, then kept pace as he continued to manoeuvre around The Works.

'Do you even have any idea what you're doing?' she challenged him.

'I'm looking for the Everlasting Candle,' Zuni answered simply.

'By breaking the rules of the Land of Birthdays,' Silky reminded him. 'Did you even think what that could mean for Petal, Bizzy, Melody and Pinx? What if they're in trouble now because of us?'

Zuni winced. He hadn't thought of that. But he kept moving, and soon a new thought smoothed his face back into a smile. 'They're pretty tough; they'll be OK,' he assured Silky. 'And if they're in trouble, I'll help them after I find the Everlasting Candle.'

'You will?' Silky asked. 'OK. So how exactly are you going to find it? It could be anywhere down here.'

Zuni's smile faded again for just a second. 'I'm not sure,' he admitted. 'But you lot always manage find the Talismans, right? So I will too.'

'No,' Silky countered angrily. 'We don't just

'manage' to find them! We pay attention to things like my crystal. It glows red whenever it's near one.'

Zuni stopped, easily hooking his elbows over the metal support railing of a conveyor belt. 'Excellent. So what does your crystal say? Is it glowing red?'

Silky and Zuni both looked at the crystal necklace that Witch Whisper had given Silky when the Talisman missions had first begun. It was perfectly transparent.

Zuni grinned. 'It looks like we're back to my way. Let me know if the crystal starts to glow.' He quickly unhooked his elbows and dropped on to one of a huge mound of trampolines. It catapulted him up several stories, where he continued to swing and soar through The Works.

To Silky, this was unbelievable. She and Zuni had been best friends for ages. They always looked out for one another, always

listened to one another – until now, when
Zuni suddenly wasn't paying attention to
anyone but himself! With several mighty
wingbeats, Silky caught up to him. She took a
deep breath before she spoke. Maybe if she
was calm and cool, Zuni would actually
explain what was going on in his head.

'So, has your mind been going for years
and I've never noticed it, or did it simply
explode into a million pieces the minute you
entered the Land of Birthdays?'

So much for calm and cool. Silky never
had been good at controlling her temper,
especially when it came to things that really
mattered.

'I don't know what you're talking about,'
Zuni shrugged.

'You! From the minute we arrived in this
Land, you haven't been acting like yourself at
all! You've been rude and reckless, and you
haven't listened to anyone else for even

a second!'

'You mean I haven't been listening to *you*,' Zuni clarified. 'I think that's the real reason you're upset; you just don't like the idea that someone else can be as good a leader as you.'

'*WHAT?*'

This was so far from reality that Silky was certain her head was going to burst. As far as she was concerned, the Faraway Fairies didn't have a leader; they were a *team* and, as her best friend, Zuni should know that better than anyone! Silky wanted to scream this at him, but of course he had never stopped moving and was already far across The Works, swinging from cog to cog of some giant contraption, completely ignoring everything Silky had just said.

The situation frustrated her so much that she screamed, and a bolt of searing light accidentally exploded out of her body. It bounced wildly around off every bright metallic surface in The Works until it zoomed straight for . . .

'Zuni!' Silky gasped, her frustration instantly turned into fear and regret. 'Look out!'

Zuni looked up just in time, releasing his grip on a metal rod and dropping out of the way mere milliseconds before the scorching beam would have slammed into his chest.

Zuni fell on to a giant, soft pile of polka-dotted fabric, which was a wonderful relief . . . until a large metallic arm reached down and plucked him up instead of the top sheet of fabric. His shoulders clamped in the machine, Zuni helplessly kicked and struggled as it carried him towards the next step in what was clearly a costume-making process: a giant set of scissors.

'Silky!' Zuni cried, panicked. 'Help me!'

But Silky was already on her way. The

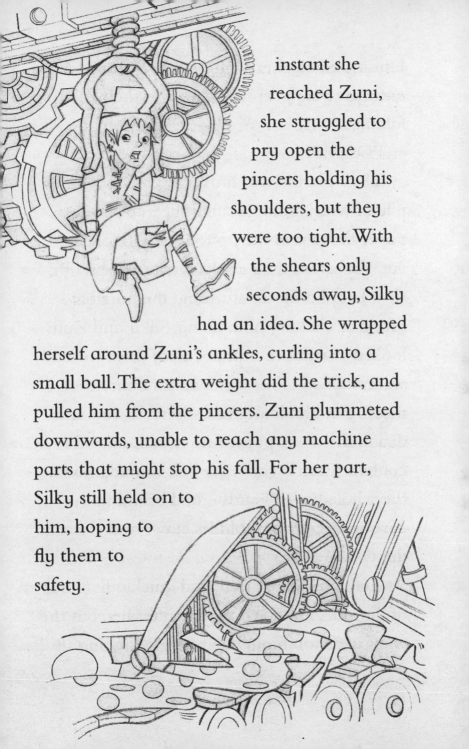

instant she reached Zuni, she struggled to pry open the pincers holding his shoulders, but they were too tight. With the shears only seconds away, Silky had an idea. She wrapped herself around Zuni's ankles, curling into a small ball. The extra weight did the trick, and pulled him from the pincers. Zuni plummeted downwards, unable to reach any machine parts that might stop his fall. For her part, Silky still held on to him, hoping to fly them to safety.

Unfortunately, her wings weren't strong enough to support them both, so they kept on falling.

FOOMP!

Their plunge was broken by an enormous pile of wide, multicoloured sheets of tissue paper that sat in the bottom of a long, deep vat. Yet before they could catch their breath, they heard a motor start and the horrible sound of clicking and slicing. Silky and Zuni looked towards the other end of their vat and were stunned to see a network of knives moving at blindingly fast speeds, slicing and dicing the tissue paper into mountains of confetti. Then a conveyor belt started, moving the whole vat forwards – and bringing the devouring frenzy of blades closer and closer to the two friends!

'Let's go!' Silky cried, and quickly flew out of the vat. Zuni tried to leap after her, but the walls were too high. Next he tried racing up

the walls, but they were too sheer and his feet
kept slipping.

'I can't do it!' he roared in frustration,
though he kept trying to make the impossible
upwards climb.

Silky immediately flew back inside the vat
and tried to pull him to safety, but they both
knew it wouldn't work: she just wasn't strong
enough to lift
them both.

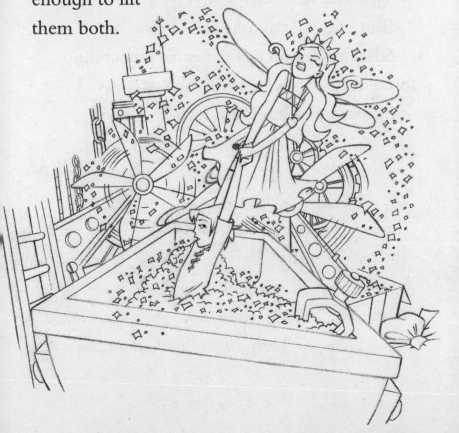

And the knives were getting closer.

'You have to fly out of here,' Zuni told Silky.

'No! I'm not leaving you,' Silky replied.

'You have to. Look!' Zuni pointed to Silky's necklace, which was now glowing bright red.

'The Talisman!' Silky gasped, then shook her head. 'We'll get it later. First we have to get you out of here.'

'But how?' Zuni asked.

Silky looked up at the fast-approaching forest of brutal blades.

She had absolutely no idea.

Chapter Six
Basic Bizzy Blunder?

'This place is in serious need of a makeover,' Pinx grumbled as she, Bizzy, Melody and Petal flew around the seemingly endless array of whirring, banging and clanging machines.

'I kind of like it, in a way,' Melody admitted. 'If you listen just right, the sounds from all the machines are like music!'

'You hear music? I just hear noise,' Bizzy admitted, wincing at the volume. 'A Colossal Cacophony of Clamorous Clangs.'

'That's funny . . . I was going to say it sounds quiet,' Petal added. 'I'm so used to hearing plants and animals talking to each other, but here — nothing.' She looked around, then raised her voice and shouted, 'Silky! Zuni!'

The other fairies joined her. They'd been calling for their friends every few minutes since they entered The Works, but no matter how loudly they yelled, the only response was the echo of their own words.

'I just can't believe the two of them would leave us like that,' Pinx complained as they continued their search. 'What were they thinking?'

'It's not easy for Zuni,' Petal sympathised. 'I bet he's feeling a lot of pressure to do something big on what could be his only mission.'

'Congratulations to him, then,' Pinx noted sarcastically. 'He did something *huge*; he ruined the whole thing!'

'Even if he did make a mistake, getting angry about it won't help things,' Melody countered.

'*If* he made a mistake?' Pinx railed, wheeling on Melody.

Melody wilted inwardly under Pinx's glare, but she held her position. 'I'm saying I don't care what they were thinking. I still just want Silky and Zuni back with us.'

'That's perfect!' Bizzy cried, her face lighting up with the excitement of her idea, 'Why don't I just magic Silky and Zuni here!'

'Your spell won't bounce off all the bright metal, will it?' Pinx asked.

'It could,' Bizzy admitted, 'but I could try to adjust for that. It's worked before. The bigger problem is moving a living creature. It's Crazily Complicated Conjuring, but I think maybe my magic is strong enough to try it.'

'You should,' Melody urged supportively.

'Or just try for *one* of them,' Petal suggested. 'If you do one at a time, maybe it won't be as hard.'

'Perfect,' agreed Bizzy. 'I'll do a Super-Stupendous Spell to get us Silky!' Bizzy concentrated, closing her eyes and raising her arms in the air, clanging and jangling her bracelets down to her elbows. She relaxed with a long breath and let her mind clear of everything except her goal. Then she cried, 'Silkalicious, stalkalacious, gettee, gettles, getz!'

'   In the blink of an eye, Bizzy, Petal, Melody and Pinx vanished . . . and reappeared in the corner of a cardboard box the size of a house. The top was open to The Works, while the floor was covered in leaves, and several pumpkin-sized ovals lay in piles in the corners. However, the fairies could only vaguely make all this out because they were seeing everything through the soft, stringy webbing in which they were completely – and hopelessly – tangled.

'Where *are* we?' asked Melody. 'What happened?'

'Bit of a Bizzy Blunder, no doubt,' replied Bizzy, struggling to move her hands from the awkward positions they were in. 'But I don't

understand it at all. I wanted to get us Silky, and instead we're all tied up!'

'And these aren't just any old ties,' Pinx mused, rubbing her fingers across the strings that bound her wrists together. 'I know what this is. It's . . .'

'Aha!' Petal cried in excitement, despite the fact that she was lying on the floor uncomfortably.

'What?' Melody asked.

'Everyone in the Land of Birthdays was so sure living creatures couldn't survive in The Works, but look!' Since her fingers were too tangled to point, Petal jutted her chin towards a far corner of the box where two long white tubular bodies cuddled together, fast asleep.

'Ew!' Melody cried automatically, then tried to soften her reaction under Petal's unhappy glare. 'Um . . . are those . . . giant *worms*?'

'Yes!' Pinx shouted happily, taking them all by surprise. Pinx was usually no fan of creepy-crawlies, especially creepy-crawlies twice as large as the fairies themselves. But now she was absolutely delighted. 'Bizzy, you didn't blunder at all! You *did* get us silky! Those are silkworms, the round things in the corners are silkworm eggs, and we're tangled in the thickest, softest raw silk ever!'

'The Works must harvest the silk after the worms hatch into moths and use it to make

clothes for the Land of Birthdays,' Petal
realised.

'No *way* do they do this silk justice,' Pinx
declared. 'When we get out of here, I'm using
it to make us the most fabulacious gowns ever
created! They'll be blinding in their gorgeous
magnificence!'

'Um . . . Pinx?' Melody said softly, 'You
might want to keep your voice down a little. I
think you're waking someone.'

She darted her eyes to the far corner of the
box, where the larger of the two silkworms
was indeed stirring. Like all silkworms, it
really wasn't a worm at all, but a caterpillar.
Its body had three pairs of legs on the front
half of its body and four more pairs further
back. The front tapered into a small head,
with tiny pinprick eyes and a snout of sorts
flanked by pointy, jutting jaws. Had the
silkworm not been twice her size, Melody
could see how it could be fascinating – maybe

even charming.

But it *was* twice her size. And it looked . . . It looked . . .

'It looks Hideously Horribly Hungry!' Bizzy whispered suddenly.

It was true. The silkworm had reared up on its back half, looking around its box. It pawed at the air with its front legs while its jaws snapped quickly and eagerly, clicking like rain on a roof. Then it saw the leaves on the floor and lunged forward, devouring one with ferocious speed.

'Of *course* it's hungry,' Pinx said, not bothering to whisper. 'Silkworms do nothing *but* eat. That gets them ready to make their silk. But they only eat mulberry leaves — that's it.'

At the sound of Pinx's voice the silkworm looked up, and this time it saw the five fairies stuck in the cocoon. Its jaws chattered excitedly, and Petal's blood ran cold as she

heard its thoughts. It dropped its leaf and
started to advance on the fairies.

'You're absolutely right when it comes to
common silkworms, Pinx,' Petal said. 'But
these are *not* common silkworms.'

'You mean it's coming to eat us?' Bizzy
cried.

Petal nodded.

'We have to get out of here!' Melody wailed.

'Yes! But without hurting the silk!' Pinx added quickly.

'Pinx!' Melody rebuked her.

'OK, OK. Without hurting the silk if you can *help* it,' Pinx amended.

But Pinx needn't have worried about the silk. It was incredibly strong and, despite all their desperate struggles, it held them tight as the hungry silkworm moved closer and closer. Melody even tried soothing the beast with a song, but it was far too hungry, and paid no attention whatsoever.

Petal leaned back and closed her eyes.

'No, Petal! Don't give up! We have to keep trying to escape!' Bizzy urged.

'I *am* trying,' Petal replied softly. 'I'm calling to Silky and Zuni with my mind, like I called to all of you in the Land of Flora. If I ask them for help, maybe they'll come.'

'But you don't know where they are,' Melody said nervously. 'Doesn't that make it harder to reach them?'

'If not impossible,' Petal admitted softly, most of her mind still focused on reaching out to their friends. 'But I think it's the only hope we have.'

The silkworm was close now, and reared up higher on its back legs, preparing to lunge.

Terrified, Pinx, Bizzy and Melody thrashed fruitlessly at their silken bonds and hoped against hope that Petal's call would reach Silky and Zuni in time.

Chapter Seven
A Cry For Help

Silky and Zuni were almost out of time. With each second, the flurry of cruelly sharp blades moved closer and closer. Silky refused to believe it was hopeless. She flapped her wings with every ounce of her strength, pulling desperately on her friend to try and raise him off the stack of tissue paper and get him out of the vat.

But she couldn't budge him. And the knives were getting even closer.

'Just go,' Zuni implored Silky, 'it doesn't make sense for both of us to –'

'Stop it!' Silky snapped. 'I'm not going anywhere without you. There has to be another way!'

But she couldn't think of a single one. She

racked her brain but, as the chopping blades drew even nearer, the air kicked up by their speedy movement sent newly cut confetti flying everywhere. Silky was pelted with the tiny colourful bits. They stuck in her hair, smacked into her face – she even breathed them into her nose and mouth.

'AAAARGH!' Silky wailed in frustration, 'I can't even think with all this confetti everywhere!'

'That's *it*!' Zuni shouted in excitement, desperate to get the words out in time to save himself and Silky. 'Silky, please be careful, but fly as close to the knives as you can. If you can flap all the loose confetti to this wall of the vat . . .'

'YES!' Silky replied, immediately understanding. She zipped into the air and flew just inches away from the madly spinning blades. Hovering there, she flapped her wings wildly. With Silky's body remaining still, her wings became a mighty fan, blowing piles of the loose confetti to Zuni's end of the vat. Higher and higher the confetti stacked against the wall, until finally it was high enough for Zuni to race up the mound and leap out of the vat.

'I'm free!' Zuni cried as he landed on another metallic bar.

Silky zipped off to join him, just seconds before the blades crushed against the far end of the vat, finishing their job. Thrilled to be alive, Silky and Zuni grabbed each other in a crushing hug. But, as they pulled apart, Zuni's smile grew even wider.

'I almost forgot,' he laughed, pointing. 'Your crystal!'

They both looked down. Silky's crystal was now redder than ever. The Talisman was close! Silky and Zuni turned around . . .

'There it is!' Silky gasped, pointing to a wall a few feet from where they stood. Locked

in a large metal case stood the Everlasting
Candle: a pink-and-white swirly-striped wax
taper that was exactly Silky's height and
burned brightly, without ever melting a single
drop. Silky raced to the case and pulled on it,
but it was welded down tightly. 'Of course – it
couldn't be *simple*,' Silky laughed. 'Let's find a
way to get it out.'

But when she looked back at Zuni, she was

shocked to see his face. His jaw had dropped, his eyes were wide and his skin was ashen.

'Zuni?' she asked, flitting down to his side. 'Are you OK?'

Zuni shook his head and turned to Silky. 'Can't you hear it?'

'Hear what?' Silky asked.

'Petal,' Zuni replied worriedly. 'I can only hear her the littlest bit . . . but it's definitely her. I think she needs us. We have to go.'

'I don't think you really hear Petal,' Silky laughed. 'If Petal were in trouble, she wouldn't just call you, she'd call *me*. We've been friends since we were kids. We live together. We've been on lots of Talisman missions together . . .'

But Zuni just shook his head. 'I hear her, Silky. She's in trouble — and it's bad. Really bad.'

Silky studied Zuni's face, as though by staring hard enough she could hear what he was hearing. 'Are you sure?' she asked.

'Positive,' Zuni affirmed. 'I don't know why I can hear her and you can't, but I can. I know it's her.'

'And it's bad?' Silky pressed, making sure. 'Bad enough that we should leave the Talisman? Even though we don't know if we'll get the chance to grab it again before this Land moves away from the Tree?'

Zuni nodded, his face growing even paler. 'Worse,' he said softly. 'We need to leave now.'

Silky had never seen Zuni like this, and she knew whatever he heard, it was serious. 'Let's go,' she said.

And, without a look back at the Everlasting Candle, Silky flew after Zuni as he bounded through The Works, desperate to get to their friends in time to save them.

Chapter Eight
Unwanted Company?

'AAAAHHHH!' Bizzy and Melody screamed, flinching from the silkworm's attack.

'OK,' shouted Pinx, deciding to say her last words as quickly and loudly as possibly. 'If we have to get eaten before I make our new silk dresses, just please imagine what they would have looked like. They'd each have been pink, of course, with an ankle-length skirt and a long train at the back that could button up to the waist for dancing. The bodices –'

'*PINX!*' screamed Bizzy.

'What?' Pinx asked. 'Do you want yours knee-length instead? I can do that.'

'No!' Bizzy retorted, then thought a second

and corrected herself. 'Yes, actually, knee-length would be good. And maybe with a little Flouncy Flippy Flair to the skirt.'

'Pinx, it's the silkworm!' Melody chimed in, since Bizzy had clearly lost track of the conversation. 'It's not eating us! Look!'

Pinx looked. The smaller silkworm was now awake, and had jumped into the larger silkworm's path before it could lunge for the fairies. The two were now locked in battle: a tangle of jaws, tubular bodies and fuzzy legs.

'Wow,' Pinx marvelled. 'I guess the little silkworm really wants me to turn this silk into dresses.'

'They're fighting over which one gets to eat us,' Petal said softly.

'Who do you think will win?' Bizzy wondered uncomfortably.

'Does it matter?' Pinx asked. 'Either way, we lose.'

'Wow,' Melody mused. 'I never thought I'd

wish for a fight to go on forever.'

Sadly, Melody didn't get her wish. At that very moment, the larger silkworm lunged down at the smaller one, sank its jaws in the smaller worm's hide and tossed it across the box where it landed in a heap.

The fairies winced. 'Is it . . .?' Melody started to ask, but Petal answered before she could finish.

'It's OK, but the fight is definitely over.'

The large silkworm turned its attention back to the fairies, hungrily clacking its jaws together. Once again, it rose up on its back legs, higher and higher, until finally it lunged . . .

'AAAAHHHH!'

'Zuni!' cried Pinx, Bizzy, Melody, and Petal all at the same time as they saw the sylvite leap through the air and land precisely on the silkworm's back.

Zuni grabbed a handful of its skin and

yanked the worm's head away from the fairies before it could strike. Furious, the silkworm bucked wildly, but Zuni dug in his heels and clung on.

The fairies winced as they watched Zuni's body snap back and forth. The thrashing beast hurled itself madly around the pen, but Zuni wouldn't let go.

'How long do you think he can last?' Bizzy wondered.

'I'll only need a minute,' Silky said, soaring down into the box.

'SILKY!' cried the other fairies.

Silky quickly studied the knot of her friends' bodies and judged the best way to release them. 'I can get you out of this,' she determined. 'I just need you to stay very, very still.'

Silky started to concentrate, but Pinx's shout interrupted her thoughts. 'Be careful!'

'I will be,' Silky assured her. 'I'll only burn the silk, I promise.'

'That's what I'm afraid of!' Pinx wailed.

'What?' Silky asked in confusion.

'Ignore her,' Petal urged. 'Just get us free – please!'

Silky nodded and concentrated again, then carefully shot a series of small, precisely directed beams of powerful light at the silk, burning it away from her four friends until they were completely free.

'*YES!*' cried Melody, Bizzy and Petal as they threw themselves at Silky for a massive hug.

'NO!' Pinx moaned. She picked up the charred remnants of what had once been the most luxuriant silk she had ever seen and hugged them to her chest.

'WHOOOAAAAHHHHH!' Zuni screamed, and the fairies' heads jerked up at the sound, just in time to see Zuni get flung from the silkworm and soar helplessly across The Works – towards the open door of a gigantic, blisteringly hot oven.

Immediately, the fairies raced after Zuni. As one, they flew over and caught him, using their combined strength to transport him to a nearby circular platform. Behind them a conveyor belt delivered a monstrously huge cake into the oven, and its door slammed shut.

Finally out of immediate danger, the fairies and Zuni took a minute to catch their breath. Then Zuni turned to the fairies and smiled. 'Thanks,' he said.

'Are you *crazy*?' Pinx asked, swatting at Zuni. 'What were you *thinking*?'

'What do you mean?' Zuni shot back. 'I just saved your lives.'

'Which you and Silky put in danger by

running off without us!' Pinx retorted.

'Oh, no – this all came from Zuni,' Silky
clarified. 'He's the one who insisted on playing
cowboy. I just went after him to stop him
from killing himself.'

'Hah!' Zuni scoffed. 'I was doing just fine
until *you* had a flash attack and almost got
me snipped to death.'

'Can't we just be happy that we're all

together now?' Melody asked hopefully.

'NO!' Pinx, Silky and Zuni shouted back to her.

'Melody's right,' Petal noted. 'Blaming Zuni doesn't help us.'

'Of course you take *his* side,' Silky said peevishly. '*He*'s the one you called when you were in trouble. Never mind the fact that you and I are lifelong friends . . .'

Petal gasped, surprised. 'Silky, I called *both* of you!' She thought for a second, then added, 'I'm not surprised Zuni heard me, though. My telepathy is really made for plants and animals, and Zuni is awfully tuned in to animals.'

'That's true,' Bizzy chimed in. 'Look at the way he is with Misty. And the way he rode that silkworm!'

'I wouldn't bring up the silkworm if I were you,' Pinx snapped. 'You're the one who got us into that mess.'

'Oh, now you're mad at me for the silkworms?' Bizzy cried, insulted. 'You were so thrilled about your Super-Sumptuous Silken Sewings that you didn't even want Silky to save us!'

That was it. Despite Melody's continued attempts to cut in and calm everyone down, Zuni and the rest of the fairies had worked themselves up to a good solid argument, each one blaming the other for turning their latest mission into a royal mess.

Then suddenly a terrible echoing scream made their squabbles dry up in their throats.

'I know you're here and I'm coming to fiiiiiiind youuuuuuuu!'

Chapter Nine
The Other Birthday Boy

Zuni, Silky, Melody, Petal, Pinx and Bizzy looked around, immediately on alert and ready to defend themselves, when they saw . . .

'The Angry Pixie!' Silky gasped in complete disbelief.

It was indeed the Angry Pixie. He was riding on an impressively large pigeon, which got spooked at Silky's cry and shied back, tossing him off its back.

'Blast you, Silky! How dare you show up here just to scare my pigeon and make him fly away. What have I ever done to you . . .?' The Angry Pixie's rant faded as he fell further and further down into The Works.

Pinx smirked at the others. 'I suppose we

have to save him.'

Silky smiled. The Angry Pixie could
certainly be trying, but he was also a friend.
She and Pinx quickly flew down to catch him
and bring him to the rest of the group.

'Unhand me!' snapped the Angry Pixie,
completely ignoring the fact that the fairies
had just saved his life. 'You're wrinkling my
shirt. And did you have to grab me so hard?

You know I bruise easily. Not that the rest of you would have thought to join these two so you could deliver me back here more comfortably.'

'Enough!' Pinx cried. Melody winced disapprovingly and, though Pinx sighed and rolled her eyes, she also added a polite, 'Please.'

'What are you doing in the Land of Birthdays?' asked Melody.

'What do you think I'm doing here?' he spat in response. 'It's my birthday!'

'We have the same birthday?' Zuni laughed, amazed. 'How did I not know that? We've lived in the Faraway Tree together for so long!'

'Did you ever ask?' the Angry Pixie sneered, wiping the smile off Zuni's face.

'Well, n–not specifically, no . . .' Zuni stammered.

'Besides, I never tell anyone my birthday. That way I can get good and angry about it

when no one comes by to give me a present,'
the Angry Pixie explained.

'But that doesn't make any sense!' Bizzy
said. 'If you've never let anyone know it's your
birthday, how could they know to bring you
any presents?'

Her lips pursed against a smile, Silky met
Bizzy's eyes and shook her head. Logic
wouldn't go far with the Angry Pixie. Bizzy
understood. She shrugged and dropped the
subject.

Silky turned back to the Angry Pixie and
asked, 'But how did you end up *here*?'

'Well,' huffed the Angry Pixie, 'as always on
my birthday, I was at home alone,
complaining that no one noticed or cared
about my supposedly special day, when I saw
someone spying through my window! "Excuse
me," this creature said, "but did you say it was
your birthday?" "Yes," I said, "but what's it to
you? I don't suppose you're here to deliver a

present, are you?" Then he said he *was* there to give me a present: a birthday party! "The most wonderfully despicable birthday party ever!" How could I turn *that* down?'

'This "creature" you're talking about,' Silky asked, sure she knew the answer. 'Was it Talon the Troll?'

'Silky!' the Angry Pixie cried, appalled. 'Do you really think I'd associate with the monster who's trying to destroy the Faraway Tree?'

'No,' Silky said, instantly regretting her assumption. 'I'm sorry, I just —'

'Apology accepted,' the Angry Pixie huffed. He thought for a moment and looked down at his feet, shuffling them. 'Then again, I suppose it *could* have been Talon. I've never actually seen him before, and this creature didn't tell me its name. I took it for a crone of some sort. It looked a bit witchy. And it fussed and fumed and blustered in a way that . . . well . . . made me rather admire it.' Though he tried to hide it, the Angry Pixie sounded ashamed as he finished his thought, and Silky felt sorry for him. She too had been duped by Talon once. It was not a pleasant feeling. 'Do you really think it was Talon?' the Angry Pixie asked.

'The smell . . .' Bizzy realised. 'The Stupefyingly Sickening Stench we smelled on the Ladder. That *was* Talon!'

'He *did* sneak past us,' Pinx agreed.

'He couldn't get into the Land of Birthdays, so he found a way to get into the Tree,' Melody reasoned.

'Just to find someone celebrating a birthday?' Bizzy asked.

'No,' said Silky, shaking her head. 'That would be a wild goose chase. Talon's too smart for that. He may have been plotting a way to stop us or even get into the vault when he heard you complaining about your birthday.' Silky knelt to look the Angry Pixie in the eye. 'So what happened next?' she asked gently.

'Well, the creature – whom I did *not* know was Talon – brought me here, and two Birthday Planners took us to a party made just for me.'

'Like Caysee and Plook!' Melody interjected delightedly. 'Every Birthday Friend must have their own Planners!'

The Angry Pixie shot her a withering glare for interrupting him. Melody closed her mouth.

'As I was saying,' said the Angry Pixie pointedly, 'they gave me a party. My first birthday party ever. Just as the creature had promised, it was a complete disaster: the bouncy castle was deflated, most of the picnic food had gone rancid, giant pigeons picked at anything even remotely edible, the guests were all late ...'

'It sounds hideous!' exclaimed Pinx, but the

Angry Pixie wheeled on her with a bright gleam in his eye.

'Hideous? It was *glorious*! I don't think I've ever had so much to complain about! And complain I did, let me assure you. I yelled at the Birthday Planners, the guests, the witchy creature . . . even the pigeons!' The memory made the Angry Pixie so happy he practically did a little jig. Then his face twisted into a scowl. 'But suddenly, out of nowhere – and for no good reason – the creature screamed "I can't take this anymore!" and jumped into a vent that led down here.'

'And there was me thinking that I would never agree with Talon,' Pinx muttered, amused.

Wrapped up in his story, the Angry Pixie continued. 'At first it was wonderful: an alarm went off and everyone was wildly upset. But then the Birthday Planners said the creature and I had to be together or we'd be blown out of the Land and banned forever! Well, I certainly couldn't let that creature ruin my good time, could I?'

'So you asked if you could come down here and find him?' Petal guessed.

'And the Birthday Planners said yes – as long as you made it to the Sunset Ceremony by dusk?' Bizzy added.

'Yes!' agreed the Angry Pixie, confused. 'How did you know?'

'That's what happened to us,' Melody replied.

This was news to Silky and Zuni. 'So we have to be at the Sunset Ceremony by dusk or we'll be blown out of the Land?' Silky asked.

'And banned forever,' Pinx confirmed. 'Whether we have the Talisman or not.'

'But how close is it to dusk?' asked Zuni.

No one answered. No one knew.

Just then, something heavy landed on the circular platform that Zuni, the fairies and the

Angry Pixie were standing on, causing it to vibrate wildly. The group turned to see that the enormous cake – which had been baking in the nearby oven – had finished cooking. Not only that, but it had already cooled, been beautifully iced by the surrounding machines and then dispatched to the platform. They watched as several mechanical arms covered

the top of the cake with candles, before the platform slowly began to rise . . .

'What's going on?' demanded the Angry Pixie. 'Where is this taking us? Shouldn't you be trying to save me?'

Zuni, Petal, Pinx, Bizzy and Melody looked a bit concerned as well, but Silky just smiled.

'Actually,' she said, ' I think this cake is taking us exactly where we need to go.'

Chapter Ten
The Sunset Ceremony

The platform rose up and up and up, until it looked like it was going to crash into the very ceiling of The Works itself. Then, at the last second, the roof slid open. Immediately, the group were buffeted by a wall of noise: loud, dramatic music, plus the roar of thousands of creatures all gathered together, waiting expectantly for something marvellous to happen.

The platform rose higher, slipping into place at the very centre of an enormous crowd that stood amidst endless balloons, streamers and strings of lights that were draped across the hillside, illuminating the darkening sky above.

'We're here!' cried Bizzy, finally

understanding. 'At the Sunset Ceremony! At dusk! We won't get blown out! We made it!' She squealed with joy and Pinx, Petal and Melody joined her, jumping up and down in excitement.

The fairies' cheers, however, were nothing compared to the ear-splitting roar of the crowd, thrilled to see this centrepiece of the Sunset Ceremony arrive.

The Angry Pixie frowned at the noise and clamped his hands over his ears. 'Don't they have any respect for those of us with sensitive hearing?' he huffed.

While the other fairies celebrated, Silky stood to one side. She was smiling, but her eyes were on the Angry Pixie and her head was cocked in curiosity. Zuni could see something was bothering her.

'What is it?' he asked.

But Silky only shook her head. 'Nothing . . . maybe,' she answered. She glanced up at the sky. 'It's still a little early, I guess.'

'You're here!' a familiar voice pealed, and the fairies and Zuni turned to see Caysee and Plook racing towards them. Caysee's skin was rosy pink with happiness and relief, and Plook turned himself into a giant blue heart.

'We're so happy to see you!' Caysee continued. 'We thought the Land would blow you out!' She hugged each of them in turn, moving down the line until she came to the Angry Pixie, who scowled at her with his arms crossed. Caysee blanched at the sight of the irritated little man, and pulled back from her hug.

'What, I'm not good enough for you to embrace?' he asked accusingly.

'No,' Caysee protested, 'I just . . . who are you?'

'It's his birthday too,' explained Zuni.

'Oh!' Caysee smiled, relieved, and her skin returned to a happy lavender hue. 'Then you need to come with me; you and Zuni each get a seat around the cake!' As she led Zuni and the Angry Pixie off to their places, Caysee turned and called back to the fairies. 'You follow Plook. He'll find you the perfect spot!'

Plook immediately transformed into a grinning arrow, and led the fairies into the crowd. Caysee hadn't lied: this was the perfect spot. From here they had an excellent view of the enormous cake, illuminated by spotlights in several different colours. They were also perfectly poised to see Zuni and the Angry Pixie, who stood with all the other Birthday Friends on the tiered benches that surrounded the cake, ready to blow out the candles when it was time.

With a flourish of music, a large mechanical arm rose up from The Works. It tapered into a small flickering flame, and lit the many candles on the cake, one by one, as the crowd

counted along, shouting out each number.

The fairies were completely caught up in the excitement, and gleefully shouted the numbers as well. All except Silky who kept staring at the Angry Pixie, then at the sky, which had officially moved from dusk to dark.

'I don't understand,' she finally said to her friends. 'The Angry Pixie had the same warning as you: he had to be with his Birthday Group at the Sunset Ceremony or he'd get blown out of the Land. But he's not with Talon at all. The two of them should have been zapped back home and banned from the Land for life, right?'

'Maybe The Works took pity on the Angry Pixie because it's his birthday,' suggested Melody.

'Or because it couldn't handle hearing him complain,' Pinx added, laughing.

'And he *did* make it to the ceremony,' Petal noted. 'Maybe The Works only blew out Talon.'

'Which gives it Truly Terrific Taste in Trolls!' Bizzy lilted.

The mechanical arm was down to the last

ten candles, which the crowd eagerly counted down backwards: 'Ten! . . . Nine! . . . Eight! . . .'

Though Pinx, Melody, Bizzy and Petal were eagerly counting down with the rest of the Land of Birthdays, Silky couldn't join in. Something was very wrong, and she was terribly afraid it would get even worse unless she could figure out how to stop it – which she couldn't.

Silky looked across the colossal birthday cake to Zuni, who wasn't counting either. Once he saw he had Silky's attention, he looked up at the darkened sky, then at the Angry Pixie who stood next to Zuni, scowling, his hands over his ears. Zuni looked back to Silky and shrugged, as if to say, 'Why is he still here?'

Silky grimaced and shrugged as she shook her head, showing Zuni she had the same concern.

Luckily, it seemed their worries wouldn't

✱ 107 *✱*

matter, because the countdown had ended in a near-deafening wall of whoops and cheers. All the candles were now lit, which meant it was time for the grand finale: the Everlasting Candle. A mechanical arm raised it from the depths of The Works, and placed it at the very centre of the gigantic cake, where it towered above all the other candles.

Silky smiled. Whatever her fears, in just a moment they would be meaningless. She turned to her friends and said, 'The minute the ceremony's over, we'll grab the Everlasting Candle.'

Petal, Bizzy, Pinx and Melody nodded, but they were really only half paying attention; they were too thrilled by the Sunset Ceremony and the glow of the hundreds of candles on the gigantic birthday cake.

At an unseen cue, all the musicians in the Land of Birthdays picked up their instruments and began to play the most familiar tune

there is. No one could resist joining in to sing:
not even Silky, Zuni . . . or the Angry Pixie.
But as they reached the final line . . .

'HAPPY BIRTHDAY TO –'

'NO ONE!' came a horrible roar as Talon
the Troll stretched out his limbs and leaped
out of the enormous birthday cake, exploding
it into smithereens.

Chapter Eleven
The Birthday Surprise

If it hadn't happened so quickly, perhaps the fairies could have done more to stop it.

It started as an explosion of confectionary. Pieces of cake, globs of icing, candles . . . they all flew everywhere when Talon burst out of the enormous cake. All the Birthday Friends were covered, as were most of the guests. Luckily, the fairies were with Plook, who quickly changed his body into an umbrella to shield them from the splatter.

Yet when Plook returned to his regular shape and began to happily lick cake from his body, the fairies were faced with Talon staring right at them, sneering hideously.

'*YOU!*' he roared, pointing to the fairies. 'This time I'll take care of you first.'

And, before the fairies knew what was happening, Talon reached down and scooped up five enormous handfuls of splattered cake. He hurled them at the fairies, casting Trollish spells on the blobs of cake as they soared through the air. His crystal flashed and, when each enchanted cake portion splatted on to a fairy, it turned into a giant, multicoloured, swirly lollipop, with its stick planted in the ground.

Silky, Melody, Petal, Pinx and Bizzy were now each completely trapped in one of these sweets, with only their heads poking out the top.

They couldn't move. They were helpless.

Entranced, all the Land's Birthday Friends and guests burst into impressed applause and cheers. Talon seemed shocked by their reaction, then smiled and bowed.

'Why are they clapping?' Pinx yelled, struggling fruitlessly to move inside her

lollipop prison.

'They don't understand,' explained Silky.
'Remember what Witch Whisper said?
Nothing ever goes amiss in the Land of
Birthdays. It never even rains. They probably
think it's some kind of show.'

'It's not!' Pinx screamed to the crowd. 'It's
not a show! This is *NOT A SHOW*!' She was
so angry she shook her head, tossing her
zigzaggy pink lightning-bolt pigtails – even
managing to make her lollipop wave a bit on

its stick — which, of course, made the whole spectacle look even *more* like a show.

The crowd roared even louder in glee. Pinx rolled her eyes, miserable.

'Where's Zuni?' Petal asked.

The fairies followed Petal's gaze and looked up to the area that held the Birthday Friends. The Angry Pixie was still there, looking even angrier than usual — if that were possible — but Zuni wasn't. He was nowhere to be seen.

'You don't think . . . You don't think he ran away, do you?' Melody asked, hating to even say the words out loud.

'Maybe seeing Talon in the Fearsomely Foul Fetid Flesh was too much for him,' Bizzy said softly.

'Not much of a team member then, is he?' Pinx grumbled.

'You all know Zuni better than that,' Silky scolded. 'If he's missing it's because he has a plan. It *has* to be.'

'I just hope it's a good plan,' Petal worried. 'With us completely stuck, he's up against Talon on his own.'

The odds didn't sound good.

Melody shook her head, confused. 'I still don't understand how this happened. How did Talon get into the cake to begin with? Why wasn't he blown out of the Land?'

'I think I know,' Silky said. 'The Angry Pixie said Talon wanted to get away from him, right? So when the Angry Pixie followed Talon into The Works, Talon hid somewhere he didn't think he'd be found: inside the cake batter.'

'But the cake went in the oven!' Bizzy pointed out. 'Wouldn't he have been Burned Beyond Belief?'

'He must have cast a spell to protect himself,' Silky replied. 'And since he was inside the cake, he and the Angry Pixie really *were* together for the Sunset Ceremony. *That's* why they didn't get blown out of the Land.'

Talon, meanwhile, had been searching the platform for the Everlasting Candle, which had gone flying along with everything else when he burst from the gigantic cake. He couldn't find it, and was growing angrier by the second. He growled in frustration and turned his attention to the crowd of onlookers. They still thought he was some kind of entertainer and watched him with rapt attention.

'Hear me, and hear me well!' Talon bellowed. 'I demand you find the Everlasting Candle and deliver it to me immediately!'

'Ooooooh,' came the impressed cry from the crowd, thrilled by Talon's commanding performance. They burst into appreciative applause, which irritated Talon to no end.

'Perhaps you're not listening!' the Troll growled, his fleshy lips peeling back from his rotting gums and teeth. 'I demand someone come forward and give me the Everlasting Candle, *NOW*!'

'*I'll* give you something!' cried the Angry Pixie, racing forwards to give Talon a swift kick in the ankle. Then, his face pink with anger, the Angry Pixie looked up at the Troll, flailing his arms and legs as he screamed, 'Villain! You lied to me! You didn't tell me who you really were! You used me to try and get a Talisman! And on my birthday! I've never been so angry in my life! I'm ... I'm ...' The Angry Pixie thought, and realised there was only one emotion that properly described how being this angry made him feel. It made him feel ...

'Happy!' he finished. 'I haven't had a chance for a good solid tantrum like this in ages! It's blissful!' He turned to Talon. 'And it's because of *you*!'

'WHAT?' Talon spat. 'Enough! Leave me

alone! You are the most infuriating creature I have ever encountered in the whole Enchanted World. I warn you, get away from me, now, and never let me see your face again!'

'I say, how *dare* you insult me like that! The impudence! The impertinence! In all my days I've never been so . . .' But again his anger soon melted away into giddy peals of laughter as he realised how much he enjoyed the chance to have such glorious rants. '. . . So overjoyed!' The Angry Pixie giggled. 'It's *glorious*! There is hope for you, sir. You are dastardly, but there is something deep inside you that's absolutely splendid, I just know it.'

Then his face lit up with understanding, and his face spread into a wide smile. 'I know what you need! You need a hug!' And, without further ado, he threw his arms around Talon's legs in an embrace.

'NO!' the fairies cried. They tried to warn

him that Talon could enchant living things when he touched them — but it was too late. Talon's lips parted in a vile grin, and he spat out a string of words in Trollish. His crystal flashed, and the Angry Pixie was immediately transformed into a small fish, but with the bearded and thick-eyebrowed face of the Angry Pixie himself.

'Ooooooh,' chorused the watching crowd once again, and burst into applause for Talon the magician.

Only Caysee and Plook seemed to notice that the Angry Pixiefish was flopping around on the ground, unable to breathe. Eager to help, Plook shaped himself into a fishbowl into which Caysee scooped the Angry Pixiefish, pouring a bottle of water from a refreshment cart over him.

Talon, meanwhile, had lost his patience with the creatures of the Land of Birthdays. He scowled down at them and snarled, 'I told you I want the Everlasting Candle! If you don't present it immediately, you will all feel my wrath!'

No one moved. They were all smiling up at Talon, waiting for the next scene in his show.

'So be it!' Talon growled. He looked up to the sky, did a chant in Trollish and his crystal flashed.

It started to rain.

Everyone panicked. Never once had it rained in the Land of Birthdays, and every creature who lived there immediately started racing around in terrified confusion. No one knew where to go or what to do to escape the droplets from the sky, so they simply ran about, bumping into one another and sliding on the slippery, soaking remains of the enormous birthday cake and icing strewn on the ground. The frenzied stampede of creatures screamed as they scattered, crying out, 'Take cover!', 'The sky is falling!' and 'Make it stop! Give the troll what he wants, and make it stop!'

Finally, in the midst of all the commotion, a single creature walked steadily up to Talon, perfectly calm. A single, soaking-wet creature who held in his hand a large candle. A candle with an everlasting flame that didn't even flicker in the downpour.

'Zuni,' Silky said, smiling with satisfaction.

Zuni stopped several feet in front of Talon. Though the madness still raged around them, neither Zuni nor Talon even noticed. 'I have your Talisman,' Zuni said to Talon. 'If you want it, I suggest you let the fairies go.'

Talon stared at Zuni a moment, then burst out laughing. 'Who *are* you, little boy?' he scoffed. 'Why, you're nothing! You have no magical powers. You can't even fly! Do you really think it wise for you to threaten me? Let's make this easy on us both: give me the Candle.'

'Never,' Zuni said.

'Fine,' Talon shrugged, and immediately enchanted the pavement beneath Zuni to catapult him head over heels, high into the air, beyond where the fairies could see.

'Zuni!' they cried, aghast.

Talon only sighed. 'Shame that boy can't fly. He's going to get veeeeery hurt when he lands.'

'The Everlasting Candle!' Bizzy gasped. It had come out of Zuni's grasp when he catapulted into the air, and now it fell down, down, down . . . landing right in Talon's hand.

'AT *LAST*!' the wicked troll crowed, gripping his prize. Then he turned his baleful gaze on the helpless fairies, still completely trapped in their lollipops. 'And how perfect that you'll all get to see first-hand when I bring home the Talisman and make the Land of Birthdays mine – all mine!' Not taking his eyes off the fairies once, he began the Trollish chant that would spirit him and the Talisman away.

The fairies looked on in helpless horror, but then Silky saw something out of the corner of her eye – Zuni! After his long flight through the air he was freefalling back down, flailing and looking completely out of control. Silky worried for his safety, but didn't dare turn her head to look more closely, for fear that Talon would turn on him before leaving the Land.

Just before it seemed Zuni would crash to the ground, he reached out and grabbed one of the large poles from which the strings of lights were hung. In an incredible show of acrobatic precision, he swung his body around and around the pole, then let go at the perfect moment to fling himself, missile-like, towards Talon, while the Troll's crystal began to light up.

'YEEHAH!' Zuni cried as he crashed into Talon, knocking the Talisman free just as his crystal burst into full flash.

'NOOOO!' Talon screamed, but it faded into nothingness as his spell took effect and Talon disappeared back home . . . *without* the Everlasting Candle.

The minute Talon disappeared, the rain stopped. Everyone in the Land of Birthdays burst into wild cheers. The fairies' lollipop prisons turned back into splattered cake, and the freed friends raced to wrap Zuni in a giant hug.

'ZUNI!' they chorused in absolute elation, 'THAT WAS AMAZING! YOU DID IT!'

'It wasn't bad, was it?' Zuni admitted with a smile. 'You know, for someone without wings.' He raised his eyebrows knowingly to Silky, who smiled back at him.

'Not bad at all,' she grinned.

'Not bad?' spluttered the Angry Pixie. The minute Talon had disappeared, he had turned back into himself and now he stamped over to Zuni and the fairies. 'I was a *fish*! You let him turn me into a fish! That's it – I have had enough! I demand you take me home *this instant*!'

'That,' Silky said smiling, 'is the best idea you've ever had.'

'I suppose you'll be wanting to take this with you,' Caysee said. She had picked up the Everlasting Candle and now held it out to the group. She understood their mission and she was willing to give up the Candle for the good of the Enchanted World. But she looked so sad. Caysee's skin was a mournful shade of navy blue.

Plook sighed next to her, too unhappy to even transform into anything.

Everyone else in the Land of Birthdays watched them, their faces mirroring Caysee and Plook's own.

Silky reached out and took the Everlasting

Candle from Caysee. 'Thank you,' Silky said. 'I know how much this means to everyone here. I wish we didn't have to take it . . .'

'Wait!' Bizzy exclaimed. 'What if we left you something just as good?' She raised her arms, closed her eyes, threw her arms out before her and cried, 'Sizzlous, sparklous, swizzle, swooze!'

A beautiful giant sparkler appeared in the middle of the group. It was as big as the Everlasting Candle, and threw stunning sparks in every colour of the rainbow.

'Ooooooh!' chorused everyone in the Land of Birthdays, amazed.

'It's a Super-Sizzling Sparkler!' Bizzy told them. 'It'll last forever – just like the Everlasting Candle! And, since the magic sparks don't actually burn, it's Super-Safe!'

'HOORAY!' a cheer rose from the crowd. Plook changed his body into a trumpet and played a little cheery fanfare. Caysee's skin had turned a thrilled shade of fuchsia, and she wrapped Bizzy in a giant hug. 'Thank you!' she cried. 'We love it!'

The fairies, Zuni and even the Angry Pixie loved it too. But, much as they would have liked to stay and celebrate with everyone in the Land of Birthdays, they needed to get back to the Tree before the Land moved away from the Ladder – and before Talon tried to return.

With a final goodbye to Caysee and Plook, the group raced back to the Ladder and back home to the Faraway Tree.

Chapter Twelve
True Friends

Zuni and the fairies were gathered with Witch Whisper in her cottage, sharing tea and cupcakes in honour of the remaining hours of Zuni's birthday. The Angry Pixie had been invited to join as well, but he'd had quite enough of company, thank you very much, and wanted to spend the rest of his birthday alone in his home – being grumpy.

After watching Witch Whisper return the Everlasting Candle to the vault, Zuni and the fairies had spent over an hour regaling Witch Whisper with every detail of their latest mission. She was shocked to hear about Talon, and so disturbed that she had spent several minutes pacing, going over it again and again.

'All the defensive spells I put up after the last time, and still Talon made it into the Tree,' Witch Whisper said, her mouth setting into a frustrated line. 'He's clearly getting stronger. I'll reinforce my magic, but it's only a matter of time before I'll have to deal with him. But things are so different now ...'

Witch Whisper seemed lost in her own thoughts for a moment, and the fairies and

Zuni exchanged glances. Was everything OK? Finally, Witch Whisper looked back at the group, considering each one of them. She smiled, pleased by what she saw.

'Tell me more,' she asked them. 'Tell me everything.'

The fairies did, raving in particular about Zuni's incredible bravery and success against Talon.

'You were brilliant, Zuni,' Witch Whisper said, looking meaningfully at the sylvite. 'The fairies were lucky to have you with them. Because of you, the Faraway Tree is one step closer to perfect health, and the Land of Birthdays is free from Talon's rule. Thank you.'

'You're welcome,' Zuni said, but he couldn't meet Witch Whisper's eyes. 'Um . . . may I be excused? If you don't mind, I'd like to go and see Misty, please.'

Witch Whisper excused Zuni and he quickly slipped out of the cottage. Silky watched him as he left. She had a feeling she knew where he was headed.

Later, Silky flew up to Zuni's favourite spot in the Tree. It was a hidden alcove on a remote, high branch, darkened by a full, thick canopy of leaves. It was where she herself liked to go when she needed to consider things. So it was only natural to find Zuni there, grooming Misty and lost in his own thoughts.

Zuni didn't seem surprised when Silky arrived. He didn't even say hello. He didn't have to.

'I messed it all up,' he said simply, not even looking at Silky as he ran his brush along Misty's soft white flank.

'You didn't, Zuni. You did great. You saved us. And you saved the Talisman,' Silky assured him.

'Only *after* I messed it all up,' Zuni sighed. He stopped grooming Misty and sat on a

branch next to Silky. 'I wanted to prove myself so badly, I didn't listen to anyone. You were right from the beginning. If we were going into The Works, we should have gone together, and we should have gone in with a plan. But that wasn't good enough for me. I wanted to be a big hero. When I think about how close you all came to getting hurt – and all because of me.'

'Don't,' Silky urged, placing her hand on

Zuni's. 'Believe me, I know exactly how you feel. Remember who let Talon into the Faraway Tree in the first place?'

'Come on, you can't *still* be blaming yourself for that,' Zuni said, immediately ready to comfort his friend. 'I mean, look at you; you've done more than *anyone* to save the Faraway Tree —'

'And I couldn't have if I just sat around blaming myself all the time. I still feel it, you know — that it's all my fault — but I know I can't let myself get caught up in that. Neither should you,' Silky assured him. 'Yes, you made some mistakes. So have the rest of us. But in the end, you did the right thing. You saved us all.'

'I suppose so . . .' Zuni said, still troubled. 'I just wanted to prove that I was every bit as brilliant as you. But I guess I'm not.'

'Zuni . . .' Silky began, but Zuni cut her off with a shake of his head and a smile.

'No, it's OK,' he said, 'because if I have to come second to someone, at least it's the someone I respect more than anyone else in the entire Enchanted World.'

Silky smiled, moved beyond words as she met Zuni's eyes. 'You know it's not a contest,' she eventually said. 'And even if it were, I'm not so sure I'd win. You're quite impressive yourself.'

'Thank you,' Zuni replied.

Silky's smile spread into an impish grin. 'However, if you *do* want to have a contest . . .'

Zuni returned her grin. 'Bring it on, Silky.'

'First one to the bottom of the Tree – go!'

Zooming at top speeds, the two raced down the Tree with the wind in their faces. Misty followed at a distance, unable to keep up with the two friends as they laughed, yelled, flew, twirled and vaulted their way to the ground.

Soon a new Land would come to the top

of the Tree, bringing a new mission for Silky and the fairies – a mission Zuni probably wouldn't join them on.

But neither of them was thinking about that right now. For now, they were just enjoying themselves, perfectly satisfied with who they were and what each of them had to give.

If you can't wait for another exciting adventure with Silky and her fairy friends, here's a sneak preview . . .

Enid Blyton's
ENCHANTED WORLD
Melody and the Gemini Locket

For fun and activities, go to
www.blyton.com/enchantedworld

Chapter One
Coming Unstuck

'NO! NO NO NO NO *NO!*'
Pinx's screams echoed throughout the Faraway Fairies' treehouse. Unable to keep her fury to herself, she flew down to the main room.

'There is *sap* in my *wardrobe*!' she wailed. '*SAP!* My taffetellas, satinellas and bubbloons are all stuck together into one giant fashion mess!'

Bizzy, meanwhile, bustled away in the kitchen, tending to countless vats of boiling sap spread over ten different oven tops, nine of which she had magicked up for just this occasion.

'I know!' she agreed with Pinx. 'We're Swimming in a Sea of Sappy Stickiness! I'm

trying to make syrup with it, but there's just
too much of it!'

'It's even in my hair.' cried Silky from the
main room, as Melody tried to wrestle a comb
through Silky's tresses. 'OW!'

'Sorry, Silky,' Melody winced. 'The sap is
just sticking it together in one giant knot.'

'So much for gratitude,' Pinx huffed,
rubbing her hands to try and remove the
sappy stickiness. 'We work our wings off to
rescue Talismans and save the Tree and this is

how it repays us.'

'It's not the Tree's fault,' Silky replied, cringing as Melody tugged on her tangled hair. 'The Talismans are its life force. Until they're all back in the Vault, the Tree can't help but have problems sometimes.'

'CAW!'

Petal's raven friend zipped into the room, flapping his left wing wildly as he tried to dislodge something from it.

Melody looked up. 'The Eternal Bloom!' she gasped.

'Oh, goodness!' cried the Bloom as the raven shook her about. 'Good birdie . . . nice birdie.' When trying to soothe the bird didn't work, she screamed out, 'PETAAAAAALLLL!'

'I'm coming!' cried Petal, zooming after the frightened Bloom. 'It's OK. The raven isn't trying to hurt you; he's just frightened.'

'You think *he's* frightened!' wailed the Bloom.

Knowing the Eternal Bloom – a *Talisman* –
was in real danger, Silky, Melody, Bizzy and
Pinx immediately joined Petal's rescue
attempt.

'What happened?' Bizzy asked, lunging for
the bird as it swiftly darted away.

'The sap,' Petal huffed. 'It stuck the Bloom
to the raven's wing.'

'Here she comes!' Pinx cried. 'I'll get her!'

As the raven approached, Pinx threw
herself at the panicking bird, but all she got
was a loud squawk in her ear and a handful
of feathers as he dodged her grasp. Even with
all five fairies trying their best, the raven was
simply impossible to catch. He was so
bothered and confused by the added weight
on his wing that he wouldn't even listen to
Petal's attempts to comfort him. He zipped
and zoomed and zigged and zagged around,
always remaining just out of the fairies' reach.

Finally, the raven flew to the very centre of

the room, in the middle of all the fairies.

'I've got him!' Pinx, Petal, Melody, Bizzy and Silky all cried at once, leaping towards him . . .

. . . SPLOOSH!

A waterfall of soapy old wash-water poured through the ceiling, drenching the five fairies, the raven and the Bloom.

'URGH!' cried Silky, disgusted.

'We're Swimming in a Soup of Soiled Suds!' Bizzy added, equally unhappy.

'And it's all over *everything*!' Petal moaned, finally easing the Bloom off the raven's wing and releasing the bird.

'DAME WASHALOT!' Pinx exploded, flying to the nearest window to scream up to their neighbour. 'PLEASE! YOU *MUST* BE MORE CAREFUL ABOUT WHERE YOU SPILL YOUR WASH-WATER!'

A kindly voice lilted back down to her. 'Is that you, Pinx, dear?' Dame Washalot asked.

'Lovely to hear from you, but I can't chat now. Awfully busy with all this sap, you know. *Lots* of extra washing.'

This was, of course, precisely the problem. Dame Washalot did the washing for everyone in the Faraway Tree and with all the leaking sap there was quite a lot more laundry for her to do than usual. So much more, in fact, that she had to set up several extra wash bowls, one of which splashed into the fairies' main room every time she tipped out the dirty water. The fairies tried again and again to explain this to Dame Washalot, but she was so caught up in her massive workload that she didn't seem to understand.

'But Dame Washalot . . .' Pinx began. Then she heard a happy humming, which meant Dame Washalot was back to her scrubbing and couldn't hear a thing. 'This is *impossible*!' Pinx screamed to the other fairies in frustration. 'The sap alone is bad enough, but a filthy waterfall raining down on us every . . .'

Pinx stopped in her tracks and stared at Melody, stunned. 'Are you *laughing*?' she asked her friend in disbelief.

'It *is* awfully funny,' Melody tittered. 'I mean, look at us!'

'It's not funny, it's infuriating!' Pinx retorted. 'How come you're not as upset as the rest of us?'

Melody shrugged. 'I just don't see the purpose in it, I guess. It's not like getting angry will change anything, so why bother?'

'*Why bother?*' Pinx echoed. 'It's not about "bothering"; it's about *feeling*! Don't you ever feel anything but blissfully happy?'

'Pinx . . .' Silky warned.

'No, I'm serious,' Pinx insisted, then turned back to Melody. 'I don't think I've ever seen you really angry. Why is that?'

'I do get angry,' Melody insisted. 'I just choose to let it go. I feel better when I don't let my emotions run away with me.'

'Well, that's just silly,' Pinx declared. 'You can't "choose" what you feel. You either feel something or you don't.'

'*I* feel a Talisman mission about to start,' said a familiar voice, and the fairies turned towards the front door.

'Witch Whisper!' they cried, flying over to surround both her and Cluecatcher, who had come to visit too.

Cluecatcher had uncanny senses, which came as no surprise to anyone who saw him. He had no less than four pairs of eyes, huge ears that stood to attention, sensitive to the slightest sound, and a massive nose that stretched the entire length of his face. He always seemed focused on the world around him, ready to pick up any change, – but not today. Today he kept squinting his eight eyes, scrunching up his nose, and shaking his head from side to side as if trying to dislodge something from his ears.

'I apologise for barging in,' Witch Whisper said to the fairies, 'but we may have lost some time. There's a new Land at the top of the Tree, although we're not quite sure how long it's been there.'

'It's the sap,' Cluecatcher explained, tilting his right ear down to the floor and hopping up and down to clear it. 'It gets in my ears and my nose. They've been clogged for days. But I've finally got them clean enough to pick up the new Land.'

Cluecatcher leaned back his enormous head and gave a mighty – if somewhat muffled – sniff. Then he nodded. 'Yes, I'm sure of it. It's the Land of Doubles.'

'The Land of Doubles?' Silky and Petal asked in unison. They looked at each other and laughed.

'The Land of Doubles is quite unusual,' said Witch Whisper. 'It formed around an enchanted mirror, so everyone and everything there is

born or grows with a double, and all those
doubles are tied to the Land. When we made
the Talismans, we took the smallest segment of
that mirror, divided it in two and placed the
pieces into a necklace charm to make the
Gemini Locket.'

'Let me guess,' said Pinx. 'It's amazingly

beautiful and powerful and no one in the Land will ever want to give it up.'

'Actually, Pinx, it's a very simple necklace,' Witch Whisper noted with a smile. 'Almost certainly too plain to make it into your wardrobe, but beautiful nonetheless. Speaking of which . . .' Witch Whisper's smile grew, taking in the fairies' drenched and soapy state. 'You might need a little help if you're going to get to the Land before it moves away from the Tree.'

With a quick spell, she got rid of the sap and dirty wash-water covering the group, leaving them clean and dry.

'This is *great*!' Pinx crowed, admiring her freshly restored outfit. Then she turned to Witch Whisper eagerly. 'Hey, can we go up to my wardrobe and de-sap the rest of my clothes? It'll only take a couple of minutes.'

'Pinx,' Silky cajoled her – it was really time to leave.

But Witch Whisper didn't seem bothered. 'They're already done,' she said with a twinkle in her eye.

'YES!' Pinx cheered, then zipped out of the treehouse and led the way to the Ladder, the other fairies following right behind her.

'The Land of Doubles . . .' Petal mused as they flew. 'I wonder what it would be like to have a double. I imagine it would be lovely.'

'I almost have a double, remember?' Bizzy noted. 'My sister, Berry. We look virtually identical and, believe me, it's not lovely at all.'

'I would hate to have a double,' Pinx said. 'Too much competition.'

Silky agreed. 'I'm hard enough on myself as it is. Having another me there to point out all my mistakes? No, thank you.'

Melody, however, shook her head, smiling. 'I think a double would be wonderful. Imagine – a friend who knows you inside out, who understands your every hope and dream.

She'd be the perfect companion – even when you just wanted to be by yourself!'

They all laughed at that, and the sound of their glee echoed down the Ladder as they pushed through the cloud at the top and climbed into the Land of Doubles.

EGMONT PRESS: ETHICAL PUBLISHING

Egmont Press is about turning writers into successful authors and children into passionate readers – producing books that enrich and entertain. As a responsible children's publisher, we go even further, considering the world in which our consumers are growing up.

Safety First
Naturally, all of our books meet legal safety requirements. But we go further than this; every book with play value is tested to the highest standards – if it fails, it's back to the drawing-board.

Made Fairly
We are working to ensure that the workers involved in our supply chain – the people that make our books – are treated with fairness and respect.

Responsible Forestry
We are committed to ensuring all our papers come from environmentally and socially responsible forest sources.

For more information, please visit our website at www.egmont.co.uk/ethical